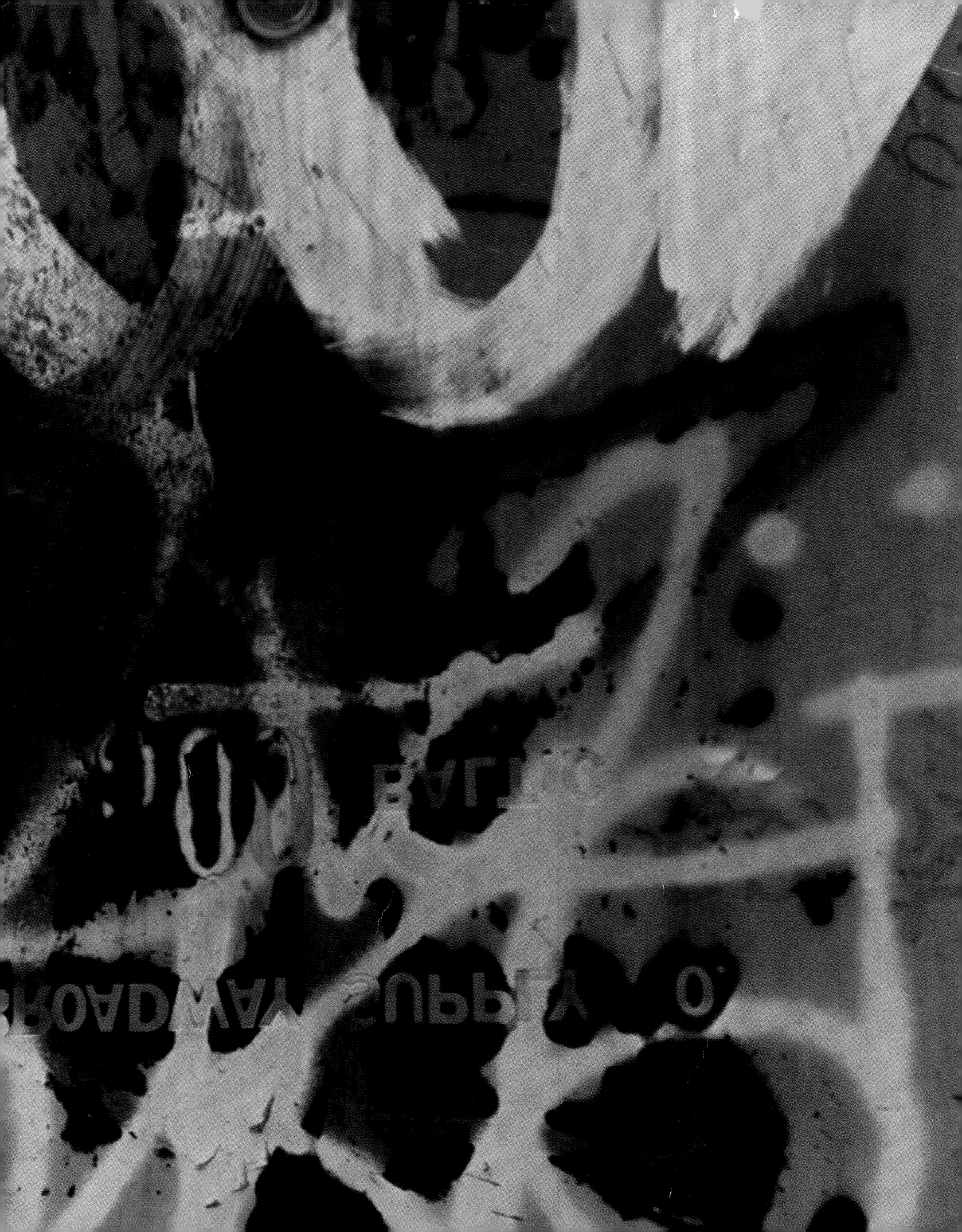

BLACK

SCHOLASTIC INC.

New York   Toronto   London   Auckland   Sydney
Mexico City   New Delhi   Hong Kong

CAT

BY CHRISTOPHER MYERS

to all children of the city, like me

No part of this publication may be reproduced in whole or in part, or stored in a
retrieval system, or transmitted in any form or by any means, electronic, mechanical,
photocopying, recording, or otherwise, without written permission of the publisher.
For information regarding permission, write to Scholastic Inc., Attention:
Permissions Department, 555 Broadway, New York, NY 10012.

ISBN 0-590-03376-X

Copyright © 1999 by Christopher Myers. All rights reserved.
Published by Scholastic Inc. SCHOLASTIC and associated logos
are trademarks and/or registered trademarks of Scholastic Inc.

12 11 10 9 8 7 6 5 4 3 2   2 3 4 5 6/0

Printed in the U.S.A.   14

First Scholastic paperback printing, February 2001

Book design by David Saylor.
The art is a combination
of photographs, collage, ink, and gouache.
The text was set in 24 point Impact.
Photographs developed by Alexis Mariel. Thanks, y'all.

black cat, black cat,

cousin to the concrete

creeping down our city streets

where do you live, where will we meet?

sauntering like rainwater down storm drains

between cadillac tires and the curb

sipping water from fire hydrants

dancing to the banging beats of passing jeeps

ducking under the red circling of sirens cutting

through the night

in the wake of sunday night families spilling

from blue neon churches

black cat, black cat, we want to know
where's your home, where do you go?

listening to brick music falling
from project windows

balanced like bottles somebody left on a wall

chasing subway mice
and platform rats

hearing the quiet language
of invisible trains

do you nod hello to the people you meet
over yellow subway seats?

black cat, black cat,
we want to know
where's your home,
where do you go?

leaving paw prints and chalk flowers

on concrete sidewalks

throwing shadows and tags

on graffiti-covered walls

leaping onto ledges
of bricked-in windows

eyes like the green
of empty glass bottles

mending city blocks cut by fences

playing chainlink games

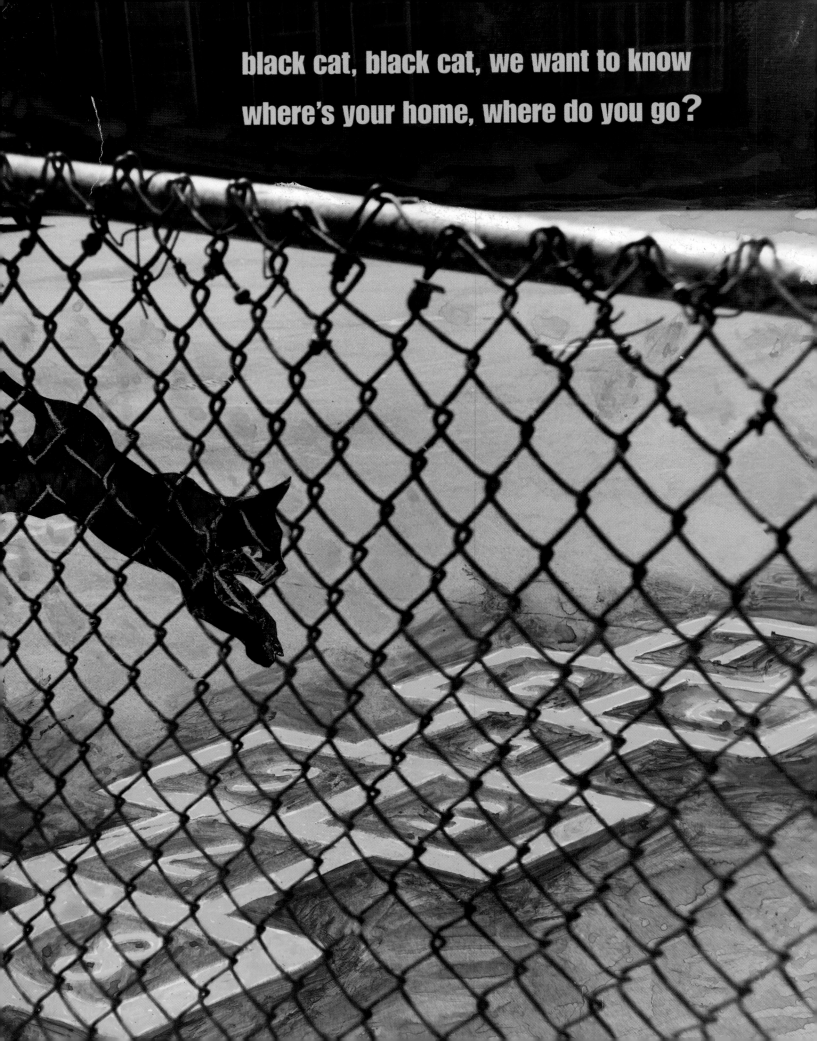

black cat, black cat, we want to know
where's your home, where do you go?

crossing basketball courts and no-netted hoops

slam-dunking yourself

through a thin orange halo

watching children screaming in playground cages

tiptoeing across the click-clacking glow

of bodega lights

scraping paint from fire escapes

edging over rooftops

seeking sun-soaked spots

on hot tar beaches

black cat, black cat,
is there a place of your own?
we want to know,
where's your home?

black cat answers . . .

anywhere I roam.